W9-AWD-007

HOUGHTON MIFFLIN
Reading
A Legacy of Literacy

Family
Time

HOUGHTON MIFFLIN
BOSTON • MORRIS PLAINS, NJ

California • Colorado • Georgia • Illinois • New Jersey • Texas

ISBN 0-618-16211-9

9-BS-07 06 05 04

Design, Art Management, and Page Production: Silver Editions.

Contents

My Sister Joan 1

The Big Party Plan 9

Lost and Found 17

What Will Lester Be? 25

Aunt Lizzie Finds Her Cake 33

My Brother 41

Eight Daughters! 49

The Family Garden 57

Word Lists 64

My Sister Joan

by Becky Ward
illustrated by John Bendall-Brunello

My name is Kevin but my sister calls me Buster. Her name is Joan.

It seems like trouble can find Joan no matter where she is.

When Joan gets in a jam and needs help, she yells for me.

Last summer we went swimming at the lake. Joan ran around trying to catch grasshoppers. She never expected to get stung by a bee!

"OUCH! Buster! Get that bad grasshopper!" yelled Joan.

I rubbed butter on her hand and explained to her about bees and stingers.

Another time we ate ice cream at
Uncle Frank's house. When Joan tried to
go outside, she let Uncle Frank's dog in.
Joan yelled, "Buster! It's my ice cream.
Help!"

I ran in. There was Joan with ice
cream melting down her arm and a dog
licking her face.

4

Last night, Mom and Dad went to a dinner party. I let the babysitter know that she must keep a close eye on Joan.

"We had better check on her," I said.

Then it happened. After a loud crash, Joan hollered, "Buster! Quick! I didn't mean to do it."

We ran and found Joan standing in
the middle of the bedroom in a pool of
perfume.

The sitter cleaned up the glass, and I
wiped up the perfume with water. Joan
took a bath, but she still smelled awful.

Big brothers must help younger
sisters, so I tried to make Joan
understand that she needed to stay
away from trouble.

"What trouble, Buster?" she asked,
as she gave me a big grape jelly hug.

The Big Party Plan

by Becky Ward
illustrated by Elizabeth Wolf

"Children, get your coats on. We're
going shopping in Willow Creek!"
Mother called.

"Shopping? Willow Creek? Us?"
The children thought Mother might be
kidding. The Chang family lived on a
farm and hardly ever went to Willow
Creek, a town forty miles away.

"Yes, we're going shopping," said Mother. "Did you forget that we're throwing a party? We will get party food and other things that we'll need. I will let you do your own shopping for gifts."

"Hooray!" cried the children, running to get coats and snow boots.

At Mister Sloan's store, the Changs roamed up and down the rows looking for gifts. Ann chose three sweet-smelling bars of soap. Chester found some yellow slippers. Joan picked out peppermint bath oil that would be nice to soak in. Paul got garden seeds for growing flowers.

"Those are nice choices," said Mother.

Mother got a pot roast, salad greens, cake mix, streamers, and balloons. They loaded everything up and started for home. Shopping put them in a happy mood, so they sang a few happy tunes as they drove down the snowy road.

When they got home, Mother said, "Let's get started. We've got loads to get done."

Mother had Paul and Joan blow up balloons. Then they hung streamers and a big "Happy Birthday" banner. Ann baked a yellow cake and Chester made a bowl of white frosting. Then the children wrapped gifts and made cards.

The next day, Father's red pickup
truck came slowly up the driveway.
Father and Grandmother got out.
They had made a long trip in the snow.
The children ran and greeted them on
the steps.

"Grandmother, we've got something
to show you!" cried Joan.

Joan led Grandmother to the other room.

"Happy Birthday!" everyone shouted.

When Grandmother saw the banner, cake, and gifts, she hugged everyone. Then she laughed and said, "This family really knows how to throw a party!"

Lost and Found

by Anne Walker
illustrated by Devin Hunt

Lee woke up early. He looked in the red box under his bed.

Sparkle, his black and white cat, had not slept there. She had been missing for three days and nights.

"We'll just have to keep looking," Lee mumbled.

17

Nan and Fran came in. Fran was munching an apple.

"Lee," Nan said. "Can you help us? We don't know where we put our new pens."

"Yes, I can," replied Lee. "Then you can help me look for Sparkle."

Nan, Fran, and Lee went upstairs to find the pens.

They looked on Nan's desk. They looked under Fran's bed. They even looked in the wastebasket.

"Let's ask Mom," Lee said. "She'll know where we can look."

Then Lee looked at Fran and Nan.
A smile broke out on his face. He
started laughing.

"They'll never believe this," he
thought.

"What's making you laugh so hard?"
they asked. "Stop it!"

But Lee couldn't help himself.

At last Lee said, "Your pens are in your hair!"

Nan fumbled in her hair and found her pen. Then Fran found her pen in her curls.

"Pens instead of bows," Nan said with a chuckle. "We're going to start a new trend!"

Next, Fran, Nan, and Lee started
to hunt for Sparkle. Lee looked in
the kitchen.

Nan looked around the couch.
"Lee! Fran! Come here!" she shouted.

"Look at that," Lee said softly.
"Sparkle's got six brand new kittens!"

They looked at Sparkle's kittens.
Three black kittens slept. Three white
kittens stumbled on Sparkle's tail.

"Good job, Nan," he said. "I wouldn't
have found Sparkle without your help."

What Will Lester Be?

by Anne Walker

illustrated by April Hartmann

Lester's dad handed him a dinner plate. Lester dried it with a red cloth. He set it on the counter.

"Dad, what will I be when I grow up?" he asked quietly.

"You like cooking," Dad replied.

"Yes," Lester said. "I can make crust for pies. And I know how to use a roller." He stopped to think.

"That's it! I might be a baker," Lester shouted with joy.

On Thursday, Lester threw three
fast pitches. Ron missed them.
   "I can throw fast!" Lester thought.
"That's it! I might be a pitcher for
big teams."

When Lester went hiking with his big sister, she said, "You might be a teacher like Miss Tuggle."

"Yes," Lester replied. "I could keep rulers, paper, and pens in my desk." Then he cried, "That's it! I might be a teacher!"

That afternoon, Lester looked at a book. His grandmother sat with him. "You like reading," she said.

"That's right," Lester replied. "I like reading and telling stories." He stopped to think.

"I might be a writer!" Lester exclaimed.

"You might be many things," said his grandmother.

"That's right!" exclaimed Lester. "I can cook, throw fast, read, and tell stories! I can be a lot of things when I grow up."

"You are something right now, Lester," Grandmother said. "You are the best grandson in the world. So try not to grow up too fast," she said with a smile.

Aunt Lizzy Finds Her Cake

by **Patty Moynahan**
illustrated by **Margeaux Lucas**

Just look at this messy table! Willy
and Pam are making a cake for Aunt
Lizzy. Today is her birthday. This cake
will be unlike other cakes. Aunt Lizzy
must find this cake first. Then she can
eat it!

Pam is writing notes with funny clues. Aunt Lizzy must read each clue to get her cake.

"Look inside a green fuzzy thing," reads the first clue. "Untie the string and read the note."

Aunt Lizzy is looking for her cake. Her first clue was in a pair of slippers.

"Hurry!" urged the next note. "Go where flowers grow. It is unwise to waste time."

Aunt Lizzy rushed outside. Willy and Pam followed her.

"Go up three steps. A gift is waiting for you. Unwrap this gift and look inside."

Willy and Pam looked at each other
and smiled. Aunt Lizzy found her last
clue.

"Go where cars sleep. Look for a big
white box."

Aunt Lizzy found her cake. Benny
had found the cake first. He did not
need to read clues. Willy looked at Pam.

"I unlocked Benny's pen and forgot to
lock it again."

38

Everyone went inside and ate ice
cream and cookies.

"I would not take a million dollars for
this day," said Aunt Lizzy. "Thanks for
my birthday surprise."

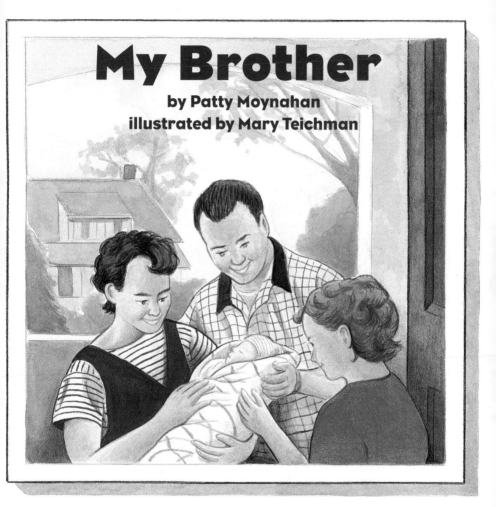

My Brother

by Patty Moynahan
illustrated by Mary Teichman

Jack Comes Home

Mom and Dad are home at last!
"What is in the bundle, Mom?"

"This is your new brother," she tells
me. "His name is Jack."

41

My new brother looks so little.
"Can I hold him, Dad? I'll be gentle."

42

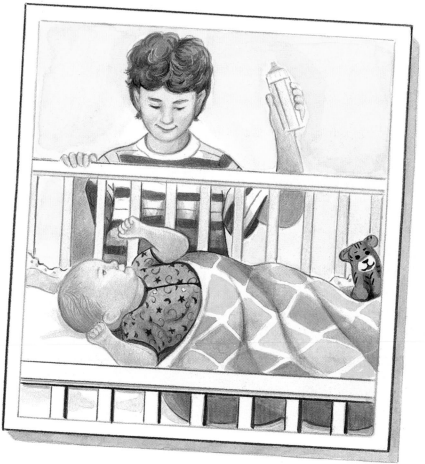

Jack Is One

What is Jack thinking? Why does he wiggle? "Jack, hurry up and talk. Hurry up and walk."

Jack sees this bottle. Jack makes me giggle.

Jack Is Two

Jack is playing with his rattle. "Jack, where are your manners? Don't play at the table. Eat your scrambled eggs and apple!"

44

Mom lets me give Jack a bath. Jack likes to play with bubbles. "Jack! Quit splashing me!"

"Time to get out now. Or else you will wrinkle."

Jack Is Three

We settle down for bed. "Will you
read me this story?" asks Jack. This
story is about an eagle. One day, I
will teach my brother how to read.

We go for walks. I hold Jack's hand.
Jack is safe with me. We are brothers.
We are best friends.

Eight Daughters!

by Linda Dunlap
illustrated by Tamara Petrosino

In the Knox family there were eight daughters. Sissy Knox, at age fifteen, bossed them all around. She thought she knew just about everything! In fact, Sissy did know some things. She taught her younger sisters how to play right.

Then came the triplets — Peggy,
Meggy, and Bessy. Peggy dressed like
Meggy. Meggy dressed like Bessy. Bessy
dressed like Peggy. Not even Dad knew
which was which!

Child number five was Doreen.
Doreen liked baking. She made muffins
for the family. She kneaded and patted
each morning. Then she baked and
baked. Good smells filled the air. At
night, the Knox family ate fresh muffins
for dinner.

Myra, the sixth daughter, played
drums. Neighbors held their heads
every hour that Myra played. She
knew how to keep a beat. But she
played each tune with all her might.
Her loud drumming made it hard to
sleep at night.

Daughter number seven was Kate.
Kate had a knack for getting in scrapes.
She fell from tree limbs, skinning her
knees. Her clothes, hands, and face
were mainly muddy. Poor Kate always
looked a sight!

Little Sara, number eight, was not very heavy yet. Sara crawled through the house on her knees. She gave bright smiles to each person. Kneel to play with Sara, and you might get a tight hug.

Now you know about the eight Knox
daughters. Next time I might tell you
about the eight Knox sons!

The Family Garden

by Linda Dunlap
illustrated by Linda Pierce

Each spring, Anna's family plants a garden. Everyone in her family helps.

Daddy plows the soil. His sure hands make nice, straight rows. It is good that Daddy is big. Plowing takes plenty of energy!

Mom and Granny plant seeds. Each
seed is placed gently in the soil. Then
the seeds are topped with more soil.
Most rows get seventy seeds. Planting
can be hard work!

Finally, it is the children's turn. Anna and her brother make sure plants get what they need. They water the seedlings each day. They pull weeds, which take plants' food and air. Growing plants need air, sun, water, and food.

60

After many weeks, the garden is
finally in bloom. It takes a long time,
but plants need that much time to grow.
You cannot hurry plants.

Then harvest starts! Anna's family
spends sunny days picking good things
to eat. Harvest baskets get packed and
heavy. Everyone is thirsty, dirty, and
happy.

Now comes the best part! It is time
to enjoy all that work! Anna's happy
family eats many garden foods for
dinner. Then Granny surprises them
with fresh strawberry pie. You can see
why gardening is such fun!

Word List

My Sister Joan (p. 1) accompanies *Brothers and Sisters.*

DECODABLE WORDS

Target Skill

The *-er* Ending in Two-Syllable Words

after, better, brothers, Buster, butter, dinner, grasshopper, grasshoppers, hollered, matter, never, sister, sisters, sitter, stingers, summer, understand

Words Using Previously Taught Skills

and, arm, around, as, asked, at, ate, away, awful, bad, bath, bedroom, bee, bees, big, by, but, came, can, catch, check, cleaned, close, crash, cream, Dad, didn't, dog, down, expected, explained, face, find, for, found, Frank's, from, gave, get, gets, glass, go, grape, had, hand, happened, help, her, house, hug, ice, in, is, it, it's, jam, Joan, jelly, keep, Kevin, know, lake, last, let, licking, loud, make, me, mean, melting, Mom, must, my, name, needed, needs, night, no, not, on, ouch, out, outside, party, perfume, pool, quick, ran, rubbed, seems, she, smelled, so, standing, stay, still, stung, swimming, that, then, time, took, tried, trying, up, we, went, when, wiped, with, yelled, yells

HIGH-FREQUENCY WORDS

New

middle, trouble, uncle

Previously Taught

a, about, another, baby, calls, do, eye, I, like, of, said, the, there, to, was, water, what, where, younger

The Big Party Plan (p. 9) accompanies *Brothers and Sisters*

Target Skill (Review)
Vowel Pairs *oa, ow*

blow, bowl, coats, flowers, growing, Joan, knows, loaded, loads, own, road, roamed, roast, rows, show, Sloan's, slowly, snow, snowy, soak, soap, throw, throwing, willow, yellow

Words Using Previously Taught Skills
and, Ann, as, at, away, baked, balloons, banner, bars, bath, be, big, birthday, blue, boots, cake, came, cards, Chang, Changs, Chester, children, choices, chose, Creek, cried, day, did, down, driveway, drove, ever, family, farm, father, father's, few, food, for, forget, forty, found, frosting, garden, get, gifts, going, got, grandmother, greens, greeted, had, happy, hardly, home, hooray, how, hugged, hung, in, kidding, led, let, let's, long, looking, made, might, miles, Mister, mix, mood, mother, need, nice, oil, on, out, own, party, Paul, peppermint, picked, pick-up, plan, pot, ran, really, room, running, salad, sang, saw, seeds, she, shopping, shouted, slippers, smelling, so, started, steps, store, streamers, sweet, that, them, then, things, this, those, three, town, trip, truck, twins, up, us, we'll, we're, we've, went, when, white, will, wrapped, yes, you

Previously Taught
a, are, called, do, done, everyone, everything, I, laughed, lived, of, other, put, said, some, something, the, they, thought, to, would, your

Lost and Found (p. 17) accompanies *Jalapeño Bagels*

Target Skills
Contractions
let's, she'll, Sparkle's, we'll, we're

The *-le* Ending in Two-Syllable Words
apple, chuckle, fumbled, mumbled, Sparkle, stumbled

Words Using Previously Taught Skills
an, and, ask, asked, at, bed, black, bows, box, brand, broke, but, came, can, cat, couch, curls, days, desk, face, five, for, found, Fran, Fran's, good, going, got, had, hard, he, help, her, himself, his, hunt, in, it, job, just, keep, kittens, know, last, Lee, look, looked, looking, making, me, missing, Mom, munching, Nan, Nan's, never, new, next, nights, not, on, out, pen, pens, red, replied, she, shouted, six, slept, smile, so, softly, start, started, stop, tail, that, then, this, three, trend, under, up, upstairs, us, wastebasket, we, went, white, with, without, woke, yes, you

HIGH-FREQUENCY WORDS

New
early, hair, instead

Previously Taught
a, are, around, been, believe, come, couldn't, don't, even, find, have, here, I, kitchen, laugh, laughing, of, our, put, said, the, there, they, they'll, thought, to, was, what's, where, wouldn't, your

What Will Lester Be? (p. 25) accompanies *Jalapeño Bagels*

Target Skill (Review)
The *-er* Ending in Two-Syllable Words
baker, counter, dinner, grandmother, Lester, Lester's, paper, pitcher, roller, rulers, sister, teacher, writer, water

Words Using Previously Taught Skills
afternoon, and, asked, at, be, best, big, book, can, cloth, cooking, cried, crust, Dad, desk, did, dried, exclaimed, fast, felt, for, grew, grow, handed, he, hike, hiking, him, his, how, in, it, joy, keep, know, like, looked, lot, make, might, Miss, missed, my, not, on, pens, pies, pitches, plate, quietly, reading, red, replied, right, Ron, sat, set, she, shouted, smile, so, stopped, stories, teams, then, telling, that, that's, them, then, things, think, throw, three, threw, Thursday, too, took, try, Tuggle, up, use, went, when, will, with, yes, you

Previously Taught
a, already, any, are, could, I, many, now, of, put, read, said, something, the, thought, to, turnovers, what, world, you're

Aunt Lizzy Finds Her Cake (p. 33) accompanies *Carousel*

DECODABLE WORDS

Target Skills
Sound of *y* at the End of Longer Words
Benny, Benny's, funny, fuzzy, hurry, Lizzy, messy, Willy

The Prefix *un-*
unlike, unlocked, untie, unwise, unwrap

Words Using Previously Taught Skills
and, at, ate, be, big, birthday, box, cake, cakes, can, cars, clue, clues, cookies, cream, day, did, dollars, each, eat, first, flowers, followed, for, forgot, found, get, gift, go, green, had, her, ice, inside, is, it, just, last, lock, look, looked, looking, making, must, need, next, not, note, notes, other, outside, Pam, pen, reads, rushed, she, sleep, slippers, smiled, steps, string, surprise, take, thanks, then, thing, this, time, three, up, urged, waiting, waste, went, white, will, with, writing, you

HIGH-FREQUENCY WORDS

New
aunt, million, pair

Previously Taught
a, again, are, everyone, find, grow, he, I, in, my, of, read, said, table, the, to, today, was, where, would

My Brother (p. 41) accompanies *Carousel*

Target Skill (Review)
The -*le* Ending in Two-Syllable Words
apple, bottle, bubbles, bundle, eagle, gentle, giggle, little, rattle, scrambled, settle, table, wiggle, wrinkle

Words Using Previously Taught Skills
about, an, and, asks, at, bath, be, bed, best, can, dad, day, down, eat, eggs, else, for, get, go, hand, he, him, his, home, how, hurry, in, is, Jack, Jack's, last, lets, likes, looks, makes, manners, me, mom, my, name, new, now, or, out, play, playing, quit, read, safe, sees, she, so, splashing, story, teach, tells, thinking, this, three, time, up, we, why, will, with, you

HIGH-FREQUENCY WORDS

Previously Taught
a, are, brother, brothers, does, comes, don't, friends, give, hold, I, I'll, one, table, talk, the, to, two, walk, walks, what, where, your

Eight Daughters! (p. 49) accompanies *Thunder Cake*

DECODABLE WORDS

Target Skills
Base Words and Endings -ed, -ing
bossed, dressed, drumming, filled, getting, skinning
Silent Consonants *gh, kn, b*
bright, daughters, knack, kneaded, kneel, knees, knew, know, Knox, limbs, might, night, right, sight, taught, through, tight

Words Using Previously Taught Skills
age, and, at, ate, baked, baking, beat, Bessy, but, came, clothes, crawled, Dad, did, dinner, Doreen, drums, each, every, everything, face, fact, family, fell, fifteen, five, for, fresh, from, gave, get, good, had, hands, hard, held, her, house, how, hug, in, it, just, Kate, keep, like, liked, little, looked, loud, made, mainly, Meggy, morning, muddy, muffins, Myra, next, not, now, number, on, patted, Peggy, play, played, poor, Sara, scrapes, seven, she, Sissy, sisters, sixth, sleep, smells, sons, tell, that, them, then, things, time, tree, triplets, tune, which, with, yet, you

HIGH-FREQUENCY WORDS

New
air, child, heavy, hour

Previously Taught
a, about, all, always, around, eight, even, heads, I, neighbors, some, the, their, there, thought, to, very, was, were, younger

The Family Garden (p. 57) accompanies *Thunder Cake*

Target Skill (Review)
Sound of *y* at the End of Longer Words

Daddy, dirty, energy, family, finally, gently, Granny, happy, hurry, many, plenty, strawberry, sunny, thirsty

Words Using Previously Taught Skills

after, and, Anna, Anna's, baskets, be, best, big, bloom, but, can, cannot, children's, day, days, dinner, each, eat, eats, enjoy, family, food, foods, for, fresh, fun, garden, gardening, get, good, grow, growing, hands, hard, harvest, helps, in, it, make, Mom, more, much, need, nice, now, packed, part, picking, pie, placed, plant, planting, plants, plants', plowing, plows, rows, see, seed, seedlings, seeds, soil, spends, spring, starts, straight, such, sun, surprises, take, takes, tells, that, then, things, this, time, turn, you, we, weeds, weeks, which, why, with

Previously Taught

a, all, are, brother, comes, everyone, her, his, hold, is, long, most, of, pull, sure, the, they, to, water, what, work

Grade 1						Grade 2	
a	car	found	like	piece	thought	across	lady
able	carry	four	little	play	three	ago	later
about	caught	friend	live	present	through	air	letter
above	children	full	long	pretty	tiny	aunt	lion
afraid	cling	funny	look	pull	to	beautiful	listen
after	cold	garden	love	put	today	behind	middle
again	color	girl	many	read	together	believe	million
against	come	give	me	ready	too	between	move
all	could	go	minute	right	try	board	order
already	cow	goes	more	room	turn	bought	pair
also	dance	gone	morning	said	two	brother	poor
always	divide	good	most	saw	under	brought	quiet
and	do	green	mother	school	upon	busy	reason
animal	does	grow	my	second	very	care	roll
any	done	happy	near	see	walk	child	soldier
are	door	hard	never	seven	wall	clothes	special
arms	down	have	not	shall	want	different	stand
around	draw	he	now	sharp	warm	during	story
away	eat	head	ocean	she	was	early	straight
baby	edge	hear	of	shoe(s)	wash	even	surprise
bear	eight	her	off	shout	watched	field	told
because	else	here	old	show	water	floor	touch
been	enough	hold	on	sing	we	front	trouble
before	evening	horse	once	small	wear	great	uncle
began	ever	house	one	so	were	guess	until
begin	every	how	only	some	what	hair	war
bird	fall	hungry	open	soon	where	half	weigh
blue	family	hurt	or	start	who	heard	whole
body	far	I	other	sure	why	heavy	winter
both	father	idea	our	table	work	hour	word
break	find	in	out	talk	world	important	year
brown	first	is	over	tall	would	instead	young
build	five	jump	own	teacher	write	kitchen	
butter	flower	kind	paper	the	you		
buy	fly	know	part	their	your		
by	follow	laugh	people	there			
call	for	learn	person	these			
	forest	light	picture	they			

Decoding Skills Taught to Date: Short Vowels *a, i;* Base Words and Endings *–s, -ed, -ing;* Short Vowels *o, u, e;* Structural Analysis: VCCV Pattern; Long Vowels *a, i* (CVC*e*); Long Vowels *o, u, e* (CVC*e*); Two Sounds for *g;* Consonant Clusters *r, l, s;* Two Sounds for *c;* Double Consonants; Structural Analysis: VCV Pattern; Consonant Digraphs *th, wh, sh, ch, (tch);* Base Words and Endings *–er, –est;* Vowel Pairs *ai, ay;* Compound Words; Vowel Pairs *ow, ou;* Suffixes *–ly, -ful;* Vowel Pairs *ee, ea;* Common Syllables *–tion, –ture;* r-Controlled Vowels *ar, or, ore;* Words with *nd, nt, mp, ng, nk;* Base Words and Endings *-s, -es, -ies;* Vowel Pairs *oa, ow;* The *–er* Ending in Two-Syllable Words; Contractions; The *–le* Ending in Two-Syllable Words; Sound of *y* at the End of Longer Words; Prefix *un–;* Base Words and Endings *–ed, –ing* (Double Final Consonant); Silent Consonants *gh, kn, b*